Don Juan Velociraptor

Lola Faust

ISBN: 9798865885337

DEDICATION

For everyone who's ever known
lust at first sight…

CONTENTS

DON JUAN VELOCIRAPTOR	6
9 ½ VELOCIRAPTORS	76
TRICERATOPS & BOTTOMS	100

1

It was the story of a lifetime - a career maker. Marian Woolridge, journalist, sat at her office desk, her eyes scanning the assignment with wild excitement. Don Juan. The ultimate seductor.

She'd heard about him in the news - a genetic miracle, the ultimate in DNA splicing between a human man's mind and a velociraptor's physique. In the year 2117, anything was possible. Science had created a way to flesh out every will. Although it was meant as one scientist's investigation of DNA splicing, Don Juan's creator wasn't prepared for the being that would emerge from his prized experiment. He wasn't just a hybrid - he was a marvel.

The scientist's assistant noticed him first. Sweet Annie,

fresh out of university, Dr. Bartley's wide-eyed prodigy who was still an amateur in the realms of carnal pleasure, was Don Juan's first conquest. When he emerged from the Splice Machine, and she heard him speak for the first time, his rich voice echoing with the timbre of a sensual growl, Annie fell immediately under his spell. They fucked for hours, each orgasm more intense than the last. When Dr. Bartley finally heard Annie's cries of pleasure, he entered the lab to see her and his creation, the Great Don Juan Velociraptor, and Annie's naked flesh laid against his gleaming feathers, both sated from their exploration of each others' bodies.

That was only the beginning. Dr. Bartley thought it must only be Annie's inexperience that led her into Don Juan's arms. But the moment the press circuit started, every single female he encountered was utterly entranced by Don Juan. He would be late for press conferences because he would steal away a young reporter and take her back to his hotel room, spending hours pleasuring her to the brink of madness until her finally allowed her release. When Dr. Bartley asked Don Juan why he had so much blatant disregard for the schedules he and the other scientists created for him, when he pleaded with Don Juan to see the formidable opportunities ahead, Don Juan would only answer, "my service is only for the fairer sex."

Since his birth, it had been said that Don Juan had over 300 women who had fallen madly in love with him and his unparalleled skills of seduction. He received gifts from all over the world from women begging him to visit them, to give them just a taste of his silver tongue and rugged, scaled skin. Dr. Bartley had offered specific warnings to all of the women in his path that he would make them fall in love, and that before long, the only parts of themselves that would remain would be those in charge of their unsatiated lust.

But Marian was immune to love. She was passionate about only one thing - her career. In the days where she had taken lovers into her bed, she had always found herself disappointed. She fucked and sucked better than any woman she knew, but still, she couldn't find a man who would give her the same in return. It was because of this that Mariian believed that love, sex, and carnal passion just wasn't for her. She was more fulfilled by the rush of a breaking news story than any man's tongue between her thighs.

Don Juan was specifically appealing. Even her editor, a ragged crone in her late 60s, felt compelled to warn Marian about what could happen should she choose to interview the beast himself. It made Marian chuckle. How much fun would it be to get an interview with the most in-demand genetically modified marvel *and* prove to everyone that his powers of seduction were nothing but hot air? It was the perfect debunking. An award-winner, if she did it right.

What Marian didn't tell anyone was that she wanted the

challenge. Not just as a professional, but as a woman as well. She wanted the opportunity to find out once and for all if she was completely hardened to the notion of being swept away in the strong arms of a velociraptor hybrid. No man could sweep her off her feet, and to her knowledge, that included any other living, breathing creature. Why not throw herself in a "sexual trap" to see what would happen?

Marian took a bite of her cold TV dinner and stared into her computer screen. An interview with Don Juan Velociraptor was playing, the sound muted. Marian watched the body language of the young reporter who sat in front of him. The woman was giggling, but Marian could tell that there was more happening below the surface. The way she ran her finger tips over her lips, the way she shifted her hips in her chair. Marian imagined that the woman was burning with desire, the sweet spot between her legs so wet that she wouldn't be able to maintain sitting in one spot comfortably. Don Juan sat back, unmoved. What could he be thinking?

"What do they see that I don't?" she whispered aloud, a smile playing on her lips. Her producer told her that the reporter in the video disappeared for several days after the interview. She contacted her boss right before the assignment aired and said that Don Juan had whisked her away to the Maldives. They had been making love ever since.

"She said that she couldn't resist him," my producer said.

"He was too seductive. Too dangerous."

Marian was ready for such danger.

2

Marian wore her best suit and a pair of high-heeled boots - feminine, but the look still meant business. She was meeting Don Juan at his hotel room in the east end of the city. Normally, she wouldn't agree to having a meeting at someone's hotel room, but she decided to make an exception this time. It was all part of the challenge, she thought. People would see her go in and out unscathed, completely normal, as if she were walking into a mundane bank appointment instead of an interview with the "sexiest being alive." It would make her success even sweeter.

Everything was in order. Marian could record hours of audio on the microchip she had installed on the side of her wrist. Anything that Don Juan said would be fair game for the world. She wanted the hard facts: what was it like to be the first hybrid with the mind and voice of a man and the body of a velociraptor? What was his chief responsibility as a miracle of scientific invention?

Why was he wasting it all on seduction and pleasure when he could actually be doing some real good for the world? Marian was sure the last question stumped him. There hadn't been a single reporter who had pressed Don Juan on his election to skip past the parts of his innate debt to science. She wouldn't let herself be so distracted.

When Marian arrived at the hotel room, she was greeted by a swarm of screaming women, all in a hysterical display of worship. It was like she was meeting a famous sex symbol, a celebrity that created such an insane buzz that a borage of security had to be summoned just so hotel guests could navigate their way through the madness. There were even some men in the crowd, yelling and crying hysterically, claiming that Don Juan was their true love and that they only needed a moment alone with him to convince him of it.

A security officer noticed the media badge around her neck and ushered her through the screaming crowd, pushing her over to the elevators that would lead her to the hotel room. A woman, noticing that Marian was being given access, thrust a small microchipped disc into her hand. It smelled strongly of perfume.

"Tell him I love him!" screeched the woman. "Tell him I need to see him again!"

Marian didn't have time to reply. She was in the elevator

and the doors had closed behind her, leaving her and the security guard in total silence.

"It's been like this since he got here," sighed the security guard. "They keep sending him those microchips with their insane ramblings of devotion. Just be thankful she didn't give you a pair of her used panties."

Marian grimaced, trying as much as possible to look professional. The elevator stopped and the mechanical voice announced that they had arrived at the penthouse suite. Just before Marian stepped out, the security guard grabbed hold of Marian's arm. His grip was soft, but urgent, and Marian looked into the man's face to see a genuine concern burning in the depths of his eyes.

"Be careful," he whispered. "He drives people to madness."

Marian laughed and gave the security guard a reassuring nod.

"Trust me, this is strictly professional," she said.

The guard looked around before leaning in closer to Marian, his hand still on the door so as to prevent it from closing.

"I know that you don't believe the hype," he whispered. "That's fine. But trust me when I saw that the moment you hear his voice, the miracle of his presence will dissolve into a different type of feeling. He can't help himself. And neither can we…"

He trailed off then, staring off towards the room where Don Juan was waiting. He moved out of the way of the elevator and ushered Marian to step forward.

"His assistant is with him if you need anything. Keep your heart in check. I was… I am…. A happily married man…"

With that, the security guard stepped back into the elevator and the doors closed behind him.

"Has everyone lost their mind?" Marian muttered under her breath. She looked out towards the room and collected herself. A large mirror hung outside of the elevator and Marian caught her reflection: her nut-brown hair gleamed under the antique overhead lamps above, and her crystal blue eyes seemed to sparkle against the sheen of blue suit. She tucked a hair behind her ear and sighed. Did it look like she was trying too hard?

"Can only be who I am, right?" she said to herself. She was a professional. She knew what she was doing and this wasn't going to let anything distract her. Especially not a charming velociraptor. Marian flashed her reflection her most professional smile and made her way to the room.

The door was open a crack - just enough to let the light from inside pool out into the dimly lit hallway. Marian heard whispers from inside. Her palms were sweating. Taking in one last breath, Marian stepped to the crack in the door and knocked three times.

3

Marian was greeted by a young woman, no more than 20 years old, who slowly opened the door.

"Ms. Woolridge?" she said, her mousy voice emphasizing her tender age. The young woman took in Marian's presence and her face immediately fell. She scowled and with some hesitation, she let Marian into the room.

"You're prettier than I thought you'd be," she said, her eyes focussing on the floor. "Most of the reporters who come to interview Don Juan don't look like you."

What was that supposed to mean? "Just here to do my job," said Marian. "I'll be in and out. You'll have him all to yourself after that."

The young woman seemed to be pleased with this

statement. She smiled slightly and gestured towards an open door at the end of the suite.

"He's waiting for you there," she said. "There's champagne on the table inside. Don Juan has found himself becoming quite fond of champagne when he gains his human consciousness. Do you like champagne."

"It's fine," said Marian. "If he insists."

The young woman nodded. She seemed suddenly satisfied with Marian, as if she suddenly knew that there wouldn't be any competition between them.

"I'm Devon, if you need anything," she said. "Please make sure to drink the champagne. He will be insulted if you don't"

"I'll be sure to try a glass," said Marian. And with that, she straightened her blazer and walked over to Don Juan's room.

"Come in," she heard a voice say. The voice was low, raspy, but with a sensual music to it. She immediately felt a tingling sensation seize her entire body and gather at the base of her naval before settling into the soft spaces between her thighs. She shrugged it off and followed the voice.

And then there he was - Don Juan Velociraptor in all his glory. He sat on a red velvet chair, his feathers ruffled up around his neck like an exotic scarf that trailed down over his chest. His legs were crossed, one clawed arm resting calmly on his lap while the other one clutched a champagne flute, the glass lightly tinkling against his talons. Marian found herself absorbed in the shape of those talons - what were they capable of? Her eyes wandered over them as they tapped against the glass and she wondered how quickly he could rip off her clothes - would it take him a few seconds? Or would it take a span of a breath.

Quite suddenly, Marian realized that she had caught herself in a lustful intrusive thought, as if it had a life of its own. She gave her head a shake. Don Juan chuckled to himself and brought the champagne flute to his reptilian lips.

"Hello, Ms. Wooldridge," he said, low and soft. "Thank you for joining me today."

His voice. Marian had never heard such a voice before. She could understand why so many people were enthralled with him, why there were so many people clamoring to hear him speak. He had a way about him. It wouldn't work on her - she was sure of it, but there was undeniably something about him. For a moment, Marian wondered what would happen if she gave into the fascination, but her professionalism stepped in before she tumbled too deeply down the rabbit hole. She reached out her hand in the gesture of consummate professionalism.

"It's a pleasure to meet you, Don Juan," she said. "I've

heard so much about you."

Don Juan smiled and took her hand into his. He looked Marian deep in the eyes and she thought for a second that he was going to lean in and kiss her. Instead, he shook her hand, but not without offering the tiniest squeeze, an acknowledgment of being taken with her, as much as it was an assertion of his dominance.

"My assistant told me that there was quite a stir downstairs," Don Juan purred. "Security helped you upstairs, I gather?"

"He was very helpful, yes," said Marian. "But he honestly seemed just as taken with you as everyone else."

Don Juan chuckled again. What were these chills she was getting, these little rushes of divine energy that seemed to tap into every sensual pore in her body? His voice activated parts of her that Marian never knew could be accessed without the benefit of another man's touch. She felt giddy, swept away, as if she were already drunk from the sweet champagne that Don Juan sipped upon. He offered Marian a glass and she took it, clinking her glass with his.

"You didn't respond to my statement," said Marian. "Do you like how everyone is so enamored with you?"

"You haven't started recording yet," he said softly. Marian looked down at the microchip on her wrist and realized that she hadn't switched it on. She always switched it on right when she got into her interviews. How had she forgotten it? Marian switched on the microchip, careful to collect herself before speaking.

"Sorry about that," she said. "Busy day. I rushed over here, so I'm not at my best."

Don Juan smiled at her and settled back into his chair. "Understandable. Please… let's begin, shall we?"

Marian sat across from Don Juan, the champagne flute in her hand idle, barely touched. Fuck it. She lifted the glass to her lips and downed it in a single gulp, grimacing slightly from the sudden rush of sweet liquor. Don Juan was surprised and he let out a laugh of pure delight.

"Nervous?" he said.

Marian steadied herself and smiled. "Not even. Tell me about how they made you, Don Juan. How did they get the mind and voice of a man inside a velociraptor?"

Don Juan looked down. Evidently, he was not used to this type of question, nor did he enjoy answering it.

"I am unfortunately not privy to all the details," he said. "From what I gather, Dr. Bartley and his team found a method of splicing human genetic matter with that of the Veliciraptorinae family. The aspect of consciousness and vocal characteristics were a somewhat different matter, and for that they never told me what the process was. Dr. Bartley is rather protective of his secrets."

Marian remembered reading something in her reports about it. Apparently, Dr. Bartley declined to give any vital information to the press. It turns out that he felt the same way about giving information to any of the scientific community as well.

"How does that make you feel?" asked Marian.

Don Juan shifted in his chair, again taken aback by the question. "I think that we all have a right to know where we come from."

"Dr. Bartley did say that there was a side effect of his creation, something that he didn't expect. Can you elaborate on that?"

To this, Don Juan smiled broadly. Marian found herself staring into his smile, at the gentleness of it, despite his razor-sharp teeth. It was reassuring and yet, oddly arousing. Marian quickly brushed off the feeling.

"Ah… the side effects," whispered Don Juan. "Yes, those were certainly unplanned. What do you think they are?"

Marian found herself lost again in Don Juan's magnetic grin and tried again to shake herself back to reality. "I couldn't tell you."

"But you can feel it,"

"I don't know what you think I'm feeling, but I can assure you that I have no idea what you're talking about."

She was surprisingly defensive. Marian didn't want anyone to know that despite all her best efforts, she was actually feeling the parts of herself that she swore she wouldn't. She started to wonder what it would be like to be in Don Juan's arms, to feel his feathers and scales against her bare skin, his talons gently scraping against her stomach, her navel, between her thighs. Would fucking him be intense? Would it be better than she had felt with any human man before? How many times could he make her cum, and would he leave her as exhausted as he had all the other human women who had fallen at his feet?

Don Juan's demeanor changed. He could feel it. But he knew that Marian wasn't ready to admit it to herself and so he stopped pressing. He merely leaned back in his chair, his eyes fixed upon Marian.

"There seemed to have been an unexpected issue with my pheromones," he said. "They were… elevated. Even Dr. Bartley wasn't sure how it happened, but when the operation was complete, and I had fully gained consciousness, I was informed that several of the female attendants felt suddenly overcome with…"

"Desire?" asked Marian.

Don Juan smiled. "Desire. They couldn't explain it, but every single woman in that building felt an inexplicable need to shed their clothes. They found me enthralling, powerful, more erotic than any other man they had ever encountered. Some of them were even upset by this discovery - I let them be. But the ones who threw themselves to the flames of lust sought me out once the laboratory was closed and…"

"They asked you to fuck them?"

Don Juan laughed. "I am but a humble servant of desire."

Marian looked down at her empty champagne flute and suddenly wished she had more. She wondered how many women Don Juan could satisfy at the same time - two? Three? More? An image of a fantastical orgy with dozens of women all screaming in pleasure flashed into her mind, Don Juan Velociraptor in the center of it all, admiring his work with dreamy delight. She shifted her hips and realized that she was incredibly wet.

"But do you believe that you owe humanity more?" she said finally.

Don Juan looked perplexed. "What do you mean?"

"I mean you're a scientific marvel. You are the first of

your kind. Most scientists have only dreamed of bringing a dinosaur back, but here you are. And not only that, but you have the consciousness of a human - the ability to think and speak and act in the interest of humanity. Why are you choosing to waste it on sex? Don't you believe that the world deserves more from you?"

At this, Don Juan became sad. Marian had hit a sensitive spot, whether she wanted to or not. She looked into Don Juan's eyes and was overcome with remorse at her question, but he put his clawed hand up for silence and raised the remainder of the champagne to his lips.

"I believe that my role in the world depends only on the demand of those within it," he said. "The demand, as it is, has been to satisfy the long-standing desires of women who have wanted to feel loved again. They ache for the pangs of true, unbridled passion to enter their lives and make them be born anew. It's what I truly believe I was put on this Earth to do. And I'm sorry that others don't see it that way."

Marian nodded and quickly shut her microchip off. "I'm sorry about that last question," she said.

Don Juan smiled, a slight chagrin creeping across his scaled lips. "Not to worry. You're only doing your job."

She smiled and got up from her place. Yes, she was

completely wet. Despite her best intentions, Don Juan had creeped into her psyche and inspired a lustful longing that she had buried for longer than she could remember. Marian staggered for a moment before collecting herself again. She wouldn't let him win.

"I want to thank you for doing this interview," she said. "It must be difficult answering some of these questions."

Don Juan nodded. "Of course. Are you sure you have everything you need?"

It suddenly occurred to Marian that she may have cut the interview short, but she refused to admit fault. "Yes. This is a standard interview for me so I should have everything I need for the article."

Marian approached Don Juan and extended her hand. She was again struck by his presence, his stature, his grace. Was it the pheromones? It seemed to be such a simple explanation, but even science couldn't explain the way she was feeling. How could such a short meeting activate a deeper longing than she had ever known in all her lifetime? Don Juan took her hand and she shook it, trying her best to retain her professionalism.

"Thank you for your time," said Marian. "We'll be in touch when the article is ready to hit the presses."

Don Juan smiled gently and she felt like she was falling. "Of course. And thank you, Ms. Woolridge. I loved speaking with you."

Marian abruptly let go of Don Juan's grasp and turned away from him. No, she wouldn't let it happen. She would not look back and she would not give in to her feelings.

Devon was waiting for her at the doorway of the suite. She looked pleased but surprised that Marian was back, as if she expected the reporter to be whisked away into carnal delight like every other woman Don Juan encountered.

"Back so soon," she said. "How was the interview?"

Professionalism took hold and Marian nodded, seemingly unphased. "I got everything I needed. Thank you for your hospitality."

Devon seemed unsure about Marian's aloofness, but she seemed pleased nevertheless. She opened the door that led to the hallway.

"Please be sure to send me a copy of the article when it's finished," said Devon. "I'm very curious to see what was said."

"You'll be the first person to know," said Marian. And as she stepped into the hallway and the security guard ushered her towards the elevator, she swore that she saw Devon pulling up her skirt, a triumphant smile spreading across her lips.

Marian got home and immediately slunk into bed. She felt like she was in a daze, as if she had been fucking for days and she had just begun to slip back into her reality. She wanted so badly to believe that it was all in her head - that all of this fog was merely from a long day and a lack of sleep the night before. But she couldn't face the reality - Don Juan Velociraptor was in her head.

Maybe it was the pheromones. The scientific explanation could make sense, especially to anyone who didn't understand the intricacies of what it would mean to create such a hybrid. Maybe it was the hype - that part was undeniable. Marian was always the kind of person who prided herself into not buying into hysteria of any kind, but there was something about hearing all of those women screaming his name that made her wonder, deep down, what she was missing.

Simpler still, maybe it was that she was lonely. Despite what could be constituted as a gloriously slutty past, Marian hadn't had sex in what felt like an eternity. The only company she had was her two trusty vibrators. Up until that day, until that meeting, she had convinced herself that's all that she needed. And yet, despite her best intentions, Marian found herself becoming accurately aware of how chronically untouched she was - and how much she wished she could change that. But she had never found someone she deemed worthy, no one who enthralled her or made her fall into the throes of passion - until that day.

Now in bed, Marian began to wonder what it would feel

like to be with Don Juan in the way that he had with so many women, what it would be like to hear his voice in her ear, his hot breath on the nape of her neck as she waited with anticipation for his hands to wander down her back, across her waist, down all the way to that sweetest spot between her legs.

Dangerous. It was dangerous in more ways than one - dangerous for her heart, for certain. She had spent so long suppressing everything that if she were to open up now, it may cause her to crumble eternally. That was the first thing that she thought of. Could she finally let herself and give into the feelings that she had spent so long pushing aside? She had been hurt before - badly hurt. Could she really afford to go through all of it again?

Then there were the physical dangers. Feeling Don Juan's hands would not come without the threat of his razor-sharp talons tearing apart her flesh. It was a real concern, and yet, he had avoided harming anyone else - Marian realized that he must be a gentle, tender lover. But the threat of danger was extremely erotic to her. The mere thought of Don Juan being able to slash her to bits, but actively choosing not to, made Marian wetter than she had ever been before.

She couldn't contain herself any longer. Marian reached into the night table beside her and fumbled around for the large, green vibrator that had been her constant companion on all those lonely nights. No one needed to know. She let out a passionate moan as she thrust the vibrator inside her. No need for lube - she was so wet that the massive thing slipped inside with minimal effort and when she turned it on and began thrusting it in and out, she could feel the intensity building to such a pitch that she moaned in pleasure.

Marian could only think of Don Juan. Even when she tried to turn her mind to something else, her body would only respond to the thought of him being inside her - slowly at first, feeling every part of her and exploring the depths of her body, then faster, thrusting with more urgency, the fever increasing, the passion becoming nearly unbearable until it all erupted into a cataclysmic erosion.

Marian's hips arched towards the ceiling as she came, her body spilling over from the most intense orgasm she'd had in what felt like an eternity. She let out one last moan and then lay motionless on the bed, exhausted from her passions, her eyes fixed on the ceiling as her heart slowed its rhythms. She was immediately embarrassed. How could she allow herself to fall so deeply into this insanity? It wasn't supposed to happen. She *promised* herself that it wasn't going to happen. But here she was. Don Juan hadn't even touched her but she was already under his spell.

"No one has to know," Marian whispered to herself. She cleaned off the vibrator and threw it back into the drawer. No one needed to know. She was going to get up and shower and go to bed and tomorrow, she would go back to her regular life. She would write the article as she was meant to, telling the tale of a genetic marvel that refused to acknowledge its role in humanity to make a difference in the scientific community, who refused to abide by the scientists' expectations for him and use his mind for the benefit of humankind. The story of a selfish being who was more inspired to fuck than he was to truly help. Marian knew that this was the story that needed to be told. *No one needed to know.*

And while she showered and prepared for sleep, Marian made herself all but forget. She moved through the rest of the evening as if nothing had happened, as if she'd never been inspired to give herself pleasure by the thought of her most forbidden fruit. A normal night to make for a normal day tomorrow. Even when she had fallen into a deep slumber and the thoughts of Don Juan Velociraptor threatened to overtake her again, Marian had safely repressed her passion so much that she fooled herself into thinking that every day after that one would be as normal and uneventful as it had always been.

4

The computer screen stared into Marian, blank and foreboding. Marian never had writer's block before, but today, of all days, when she had one of the world's most impressive stories and an editor that was demanding a quick turnaround, she couldn't write a word. The blank screen mirrored the fogginess in her mind, the insufferable creative block that refused to let her progress. She had everything she needed - why was it so hard to put the story into words?

Marian jumped as she heard a loud buzzing beside her. Her phone, which she had somehow forgotten to put on silent, was ringing off the hook. She sighed and looked at the caller ID. Unknown number. She was about to let it go to voicemail when she suddenly had a feeling that this call was going to be important.

At the last moment, Marian grabbed the phone.

"Hello?" she said.

There was a pause and then a small voice said, "Ms. Woolridge?"

"Yes?"

Another long pause. It was as if the person calling didn't want to be on the phone at all.

"Ms. Woolridge, this is Devon. Don Juan's assistant. I was wondering if I could have a moment of your time?"

Marian nearly dropped the phone in shock. "What can I do for you, Devon?" she said.

Devon sighed. "Don Juan felt like your conversation was… cut short yesterday. He was wondering if you would meet with him again."

Marian was speechless. "Meet again? Why?"

"Like I said, he felt like your meeting was cut short."

Her heart leapt. Marian couldn't tell if it was elation or nerves that had seized her, but she knew that the news of Don Juan's request could not be ignored.

"Wh… where does he want to meet me?"

Devon took another pause. Marian could tell that she did not want to make this call, and was probably starting to even regret her decision to work for Don Juan.

"He has a vacation home in the Maldives. Dr. Bartley used it for research, but he's since gifted it to Don Juan. We can have a private jet meet you at the airport where you'll be taken directly to his private airspace. All expenses paid."

Marian could barely contain her excitement, but she quickly swallowed it down for the sake of her professional image. "If he's willing to pay the expenses, I guess I can't say no."

"Good," said Devon. "The plane will leave at 7:45 am. We'll have someone come get you and drive you to the airport at 5:30 am sharp. Be ready."

Marian was about to thank her when Devon hung up the phone unceremoniously. Marian didn't care. The excitement that was broiling in the pit of her stomach was too strong to ignore. He *requested* her. Another meeting meant more material, more stories. The blank computer screen that stared back at her wouldn't be bare for long. By the end of this next meeting, Marian would have pried out so many stories that her editor would practically be swooning from the weight of her genius. It was the perfect opportunity to double down on her success.

Still, there was a separate sensation, a fluttering in her

stomach that tickled her all the way to her most intimate spots that told her that there was something else to be excited for. Could the fantasy be just as good as the reality? Marian found herself wondering this as she began to pack her things in her suitcase. Was there a part of her, a small part maybe, that wanted to see if the real thing was as good as what she had imagined?

Under the clarity of the day, Marian was still ready to write off her urges as nothing but a passing fancy, a summation of her loneliness and her thirst for adventure. But there was another part of her that was undeniably aroused. The thought of danger, of the physical and emotional sensation that could fill her to the brim with pleasure was almost more exciting to her than the story itself. She would never admit it to anyone, and she would barely admit it to herself, but Marian was so sexually charged by the idea of getting to experience Don Juan for herself that she was physically buzzing.

The jet was like something out of a magazine - leather seating, glossy finish on the wooden chairs, and the crisp scent of champagne on ice. The flight attendant greeted her cheerily and ushered Marian to her seat - more luxurious than any armchair she had sat in before, its decorative structure giving the impression of a throne more than an airplane seat. Without even asking, the flight attendant popped the champagne bottle and poured Marian a glass. A bowl of ripe, red strawberries and whipped cream seemingly appeared beside her and Marian gasped with unfettered delight. The flight attendant giggled.

"Only the best for Don Juan's esteemed guests," said the flight attendant.

Marian grinned, ear to ear, and popped a strawberry into her mouth. Perfect. The texture traced her lips as the sweet juices hit her tongue, the whipped cream teasing the symphonic flavor in a playful melody. A tiny spec of whipped cream remained at the corner of her lip and the flight attendant took it upon herself to wipe it away. Marian was surprised at the gesture, but also intrigued at the inherent sensuality of it.

"Aren't we supposed to wait until the plane takes off before we have, ugh…. Refreshments?"

The flight attendant beamed. "There are no rules here," she said, giving Marian a coy little wink. "You'll find that here. Everything Don Juan touches comes with a bit of… extra spice."

Marian had never been the type to decipher when someone was flirting with her, but she noted a definite flirty tone in this flight attendant. The woman was right - it seemed as though everything that touched Don Juan was tinged in eroticism, as if his entire existence was the basis for the ultimate fantasy. Marian watched as the flight attendant bit her lip suggestively before walking to the front of the plane, taking her seat for takeoff.

"This is all *so* weird," Marian thought to herself as the plane sped up and took off into the clouds. Yet there was a part of her that was really enjoying it. Didn't she deserve a little adventure? After so many years of boredom and lackluster romance, didn't she deserve a little wink and a glass of champagne every once in a while? She took a sip and immediately fell into a lustful daydream. Whatever was about to happen to her, Marian was now sure that she was going to have the time of her life.

5

The plane landed at the edge of one of the most beautiful beaches she had ever seen - definitely worth the exhausting journey it had taken to get there. Marian looked out into the early morning sunlight and smiled - she was in paradise. Though her mind was still foggy from too much champagne and her body was weighed down by too much delicious gourmet food, Marian felt a joy and weightlessness that she had never encountered before. Pure ecstatic expectation engulfed her, surrounding her entire form with the promise of a new adventure. Was she even prepared for what was about to happen? Marian laughed to herself - there was likely nothing in the world that could prepare her for what the day would hold.

A sleek Mercedes Benz met her at the beachside airfield and whisked her away through the island, passing a barrage of white sand beaches kissed with aquamarine waters. The driver, a kindly man in his late 60s, explained to her that there would be more crystal waters at the marina near the villa where she would be staying. The swimming was perfect, he said, and Don Juan had already made special arrangements that she could swim at any time she wished. He had even arranged a scuba diving lesson for her, should that interest her. Marian was impressed with how well Don Juan had arranged everything and was thrilled at the idea of diving below the crystalline waters.

The car pulled up to a sprawling villa - an open-aired luxury structure that looked like it had been snatched directly from a travel magazine. Marian stepped out to admire her accommodations. She had never dreamed that she would have the opportunity to witness something so beautiful, let alone stay the night! Before she had arrived, Devon had let her know that Marian was invited to spend a few days, and despite her best judgment, Marion agreed. After all, when would she have the next opportunity to stay in a luxury villa?

Something in the corner of her eye caught her attention. It was a pristine, white coat in the distance, descending from a stairwell at the east entrance and walking towards her. Marian shielded her eyes to make out the figure approaching her. The man continued his approach and Marian suddenly realized that the man was a scientist. There was only one person this man could be.

"Marian Woolridge," said the scientist, extending his hand. "My name is Dr. Bartley. Pleased to meet you."

Marian took his hand with some hesitation. She was not expecting to see any of the scientists that day, but before she could completely rebuke the idea, she realized that she didn't actually know what to expect. Dr. Bartley smiled at her, but the smile was cold, devoid of any sincerity or genuine kindness.

"Nice to meet you," said Marian. "To what do I owe this pleasure?"

Dr Bartley laughed mirthlessly and began to lead Marian up to the villa. "I happen to be here conducting some tests. We are in the middle of recording some valuable new discoveries pertaining to Don Juan."

"I thought this villa had been gifted to him by you," said Marian.

Dr. Bartley laughed again. "Yes, it has. But occasionally, research takes priority. Don Juan doesn't mind. I'm sure you'll find the villa to be very private when necessary."

Something about his final statement gave Marian the shivers. What was Dr. Bartley expecting to happen? For a moment, Marian feared that he had the power to read her mind and see into the hidden desires that she had tried to bury, but quickly passed that off as paranoia. What business was it of his if Marian required privacy for her second interview?

"I assure you that everything here is completely

professional," said Marian. "I'm here to gather more information. The vacation is just an added little perk."

"Professional," repeated Dr. Bartley. "Yes, professional. That's precisely why I selected you.

"Selected me?" asked Marian. "What do you mean?"

Dr. Bartley laughed his low, mirthless laugh again. "Did you think that we let just anyone interview our Don Juan Velociraptor? We've been inundated with messages from thousands of journalists since we launched the news of his birth. We are very selective of who gets to see him up close."

Marian was shocked by Dr. Bartley's admission. All this time, she thought that she'd gotten the story herself with her own gumption, but here it was - the whole truth. Dr. Bartley was pulling the strings from the beginning. She shouldn't be surprised, but it was still disappointing to find out that she wasn't the one to have landed her coveted assignment by her own design.

"I guess I should be flattered," said Marian.

"Don Juan has taken quite a liking to you," said Dr. Bartley. "More so than he has with other reporters in the past. He says you intrigue him."

Marian felt a surge of excitement and quickly swallowed it down. "In what way?"

"He says you're mysterious. Impossible to read. I think he finds that very appealing."

"I don't typically open up to my subjects," said Marian.

There was a pointed nature to her remark that was not lost on Dr. Bartley - a kind of "watch out" feeling that served as a warning. He was testing her and she wasn't going to take the bait. Dr. Bartley gave her a pursed-lip smile and ushered her through the front entrance and into the main hallway. The click of their heels echoes against the Spanish tiled floors, giving her the distinct impression that even though the place was inhabited, you could still feel like you were the only person on Earth.

"Your room is at the end of the west hallway," said Dr. Bartley. "Follow the Spanish tiles all the way to the end of the hallway and you'll see a small staircase. That will take you directly to your room. Please let me know if you need anything else."

Before Marian could say another word, Dr. Bartley turned away from her and began to walk in the other direction. She marveled at how well her veiled insult had landed and made her way to the end of the hallway, as she had been directed.

The room that she would be staying in was the most luxurious she had ever seen. Oakwood floors and Persian rugs sprawled across the vast living space, which was approximately the size of Marian's own apartment. A large bathtub that appeared to be made of crystal sat before the window that led out to the balcony, the spectacular view of the Indian Ocean greeting her with the clarity and calmness of its perfect blue waters. The bed near the center of the room was something out of a romance novel - immense and dressed in gold coloured sheets, decorated with a bevy of ornamental throw pillows. A canopy draped over four oakwood poles at the corners of the bed, and Marian briefly entertained the thought of how fun it would be to fuck in that bed before scrubbing her dirty little mind clean with the importance of the task at hand.

Marian was about to begin unpacking her bag when she heard a knock at the door. She had barely been there enough time to be formally announced - who could it be? Marian opened the door to see a small elderly woman standing at the other end, her face peering upwards to meet Marian's gaze.

"Don Juan is ready for you, ma'am," she said.

"What? Already?" said Marian.

"Yes ma'am. Right this way."

Leaving all of her stuff strewn over the bed, Marian followed the woman out the bedroom door and into the hallway.

6

Marian felt like they had been walking for hours when they finally reached the breakfast nook where Don Juan sat, basking in the sun. His taloned hand was wrapped around a coffee cup as he started out towards the beach, taking in the sweet ocean breeze as it kissed the feathers on his chest. She wondered what it must be like being in his place right now, the calm after the media frenzy storm, just him and the wind and the sea. Marian was hesitant to interrupt his peace, but Don Juan suddenly turned to see her and the elderly woman standing at the entrance.

"Ah, Ms. Woolridge!" he said. "So good of you to come. Please join me!"

Marian smiled, pleased that he seemed enthused to see her. The woman turned to leave them to their conversation as Marian took her seat across from him at the breakfast table. There was a new light in his eyes, an ease that she had not seen when they had first met in his hotel room. Was it that they were shining? As he met her gaze, Marian noticed for the first time that there was a softness there, as if he were silently imploring for understanding, for kindness. Despite her professional shell, Marian felt herself softening at the tenderness of his gaze.

"I wasn't sure you would come," he said.

"Neither was I," said Marian. "But I couldn't resist the prospect of expanding this story."

Don Juan nodded and gestured to his coffee cup. "This is the finest I've ever had. My housekeeper, who you just met, harvests the beans herself. Would you care for a cup?"

"No thank you," said Marian. "I'm afraid that I've stuffed myself with far too much champagne and strawberries,"

Don Juan laughed. "Yes. My flight attendant can be quite persuasive…"

"I'm sure she can," said Marian. "Now, let's get down to business. You said you felt like our conversation was cut short?"

"Yes," said Don Juan. "I feel like you may not have had the picture perfectly painted,"

"Picture?" asked Marian. "Of your celebrity?"

Don Juan frowned. "I don't care much for that word,"

"Why? Because it doesn't paint the picture?"

"It seems nefarious. As if it's more important to me than everything else."

"Is it?"

Don Juan sighed. "My goal is simply to experience life. And to offer experience in return."

"But you have to admit, the perks here are undeniable."

"I will admit, the use of this villa, the private jet… there are a lot of things that are somewhat advantageous…"

There was a long pause. They both looked out to the ocean, Don Juan now lost in thought.

"Dr. Bartley met me on the beach," said Marian finally. "I was surprised to see him."

"Yes," sighed Don Juan. "He is conducting more research. But to be honest, I don't trust him."

Marian's intrigue was elevated. "Why's that?"

Don Juan looked around him, fearful of anyone who might hear what he had to say.

"He seems to be planning something. It's clear that he's

disappointed with the way that I have been hesitant to tout his scientific genius to the media. I think he wants assurance."

"What do you mean?" asked Marian.

"I didn't ask to be created, Ms. Wooldridge. Nothing that I have now was agreed upon - it was all pushed onto me. I have no choice. I don't believe that everything the doctor does is ethical, nor do I believe that he should continue his experimentations on DNA and consciousness splicing. Now that I have free will, I don't wish to perpetuate a world where men like Dr. Bartley can harm others while claiming praise from the scientific community."

Marian gasped. This story was becoming even more than she had ever bargained for.

"What is he doing to harm others?" she asked.

Don Juan looked around again before coming closer to her. He placed a cool claw on Marian's knee and she felt her heart leap into her throat with exquisite anticipation.

"Dr. Bartley is devoid of ethical thought," whispered Don Juan. "He is set on continuing his experiments on other beings. As a being without human consciousness, it's nothing to him to give the consciousness of man to a dinosaur. But what if he wants to change consciousness from one human body to another, without their consent? If I did not have the consciousness to give consent, do you think he will care if he gets consent in other cases?"

A wave of horror washed over Marian. Don Juan wasn't a celebrity playboy who was fucking his way through every woman who crossed his path. He was a prisoner.

"Is he threatening you?" asked Marian. "Is he threatening to hurt you if you don't do what he says and tell the world that his scientific endeavors are ethical?"

Don Juan nodded. "It's a veiled threat, but a threat nonetheless. That's why I've been living as I do. If he thinks that I'm only concerned about sex and bottles of champagne with reporters, he won't see me as a viable pawn in his master plan. But time is running out and I'm starting to believe that even that won't save me. I don't know what he plans to do…"

"Whatever it is, we won't let it happen," said Marian. She put her other hand on top of his claw and squeezed it, surprising Don Juan with the intimacy of the gesture. "I won't let him get away with it."

They stared into each other's eyes in silence. At once, Marian felt everything that she had been missing all those years - the passion, the pleasure, the lust for a creature that was less physically human than her previous partners, yet somehow felt more human than them all. Marian's heart began to race as Don Juan reached out and gently ran his talons through her hair.

"He told me you didn't care," said Don Juan. "Out of all

the women I encountered, I desired you the most. You were so hard to read, so distant. But I sensed a powerful sensuality in you that none of the other women had. You were a beacon of light to me. But the doctor in his jealousy and tyranny told me that I was nothing but a story to you. You were immune to me."

He continued to run his fingers through her hair and Marian wanted more. She wanted everything. She had fought it for so long that she would no longer let herself fall to the trap of deprivation. This was her time. Like the ocean waves against the sand, Marian suddenly realized that every doubt she had was instantly washed away.

"I told myself I was immune," she whispered. "I didn't understand it until I was in the room with you. I tried to tell myself that I was just going after the story, but after being with you here and hearing you be so open, fuck it. I'm done pretending. I want you."

Don Juan leaned forward and kissed her passionately. Marian fell into his arms as if it were the first time she had ever been kissed, the first time she had ever felt the touch of an expert lover. When he pulled away, her eyes met his again and she swooned.

"How do I know I'm not just another notch in your belt?" said Marian.

"How do I know I'm not a notch in yours?" said Don Juan.

They had reached the point of no return. At that moment, there was no past, no history that had led them to that first kiss. It seemed as though all of Marian's life had been building to this, waiting for this moment when she could finally give in to the waves of ecstasy.

"I guess we just need to trust each other then," she whispered.

7

Marian felt like she was floating through the air as Don Juan carried her back to the bedroom. He laid her down on the bed and once he'd safely locked the door, he came back to her, his voice low and soft against her ear.

"How do you want it?" he purred.

Marian thrust her hips towards him in response. "Rip off my clothes."

Don Juan grinned and with one sharp slice of his talons, he obliterated her dress, leaving the pieces scattered across the bed. Her body, soft and deliciously supple, lay exposed to him, completely unharmed by his talons, but quivering in anticipation. Don Juan dipped down Marian's skin and his tongue explored the lengths of her body.

"You're perfect," he whispered. Marian could do nothing but moan a response as his tongue ventured down to the base of her navel and between her legs, lapping at the wetness that greeted him with expert efficiency. Marian gasped with ecstasy, her body unable to contain itself as the first orgasm came, pouring forth like the sun kissed waves from the beach outside her window. Don Juan's tongue continued its deft work as she felt the waves crashing again and again, her thighs shaking violently with each passing moment of ecstasy. When she thought she couldn't take any more, Don Juan moved up to meet her eyes once more, his own dancing with the fire of carnality.

"Do you want me to fuck you?" he said.

"Yes…" moaned Marian.

"Tell me. I want to hear you tell me how much you want me to fuck you."

Marian writhed beneath him, her body craving the ultimate culmination of their passion.

"I want you to fuck me," she whispered.

"How much?" growled Don Juan. "How much do you want me to fuck you?"

"It's all I've dreamed about since I've met you. I need it. I need it now. Please."

Don Juan gently caressed Marian's face as he entered her, gentle at first, just how she had envisioned it. She thrust her hips upwards to meet his as he continued his rhythm, slowly gaining momentum, the movements gaining strength and ferocity as Don Juan continued to thrust into her. It was the best she had ever felt. Every man from her past who had tried to impress her with his prowess was nothing but a drop in the ocean for her. Every thrust, every touch, every kiss paled in comparison to what she was experiencing right then with Don Juan.

They stayed in that rhythm for what felt like both eternity and the beat of a butterfly's wings. Don Juan roared with rapture, rolling off of Marian and collapsing onto the bed, panting and gasping for the coveted post-coital breath. Marian lay back in the heaps of gold-sheened blankets, her body slick with sweat and a smile of satisfaction spreading wide across her lips. They lay in silence for a long while with nothing but the sound of the pounding waves and the wind through the palm trees outside. Finally, Don Juan reached over and clasped Marian's hand into his. She melted instantly and crept closer to rest her head on his chest.

"I've never felt like that," she said. "Ever."

"I don't think I have either," said Don Juan.

Marian laughed. "You tell all the pretty girls that, don't you?"

Don Juan shook his head. “Never. I’m being sincere. It was like doing it for the first time.”

Marian ceased her laughter and tilted her head towards him. “Well… it didn’t *feel* like you were doing that for the first time,”

“That’s not what I mean. It’s the *feeling*. A first taste of something undeniably delicious. A taste that once you have it, you never want any other food ever again.”

Marian sat upright. Could he be saying what she thought he was saying? As if reading her mind, Don Juan turned to face her, taking the hand that was already upon his chest where his heart laid.

“I can’t deny what I feel,” he whispered. “And from the moment I first saw your face, I knew I was doomed.”

A frantic knock sounded at the door. Shaken by the sudden interruption, Marian jumped from the bed, wrapped herself in a robe, and scrambled to the door. She opened it to see the elderly woman from earlier, Don Juan’s housekeeper, slick with sweat and gasping for breath.

“Ms. Woolridge,” she choked out between heaves. “I know Don Juan is with you. They’re coming for him. I ran all the way here to warn you…”

"Wait a minute, who's coming for him?" said Marian.

"Dr. Bartley and the others. They're coming to take him. You must get him out of here!"

8

There was barely time to think. Don Juan rushed from the bed and stuck his head out the door. In the distance, his keen hearing discerned a group of men, armed and ready, storming through the villa and making their way towards Marian's suite. They undoubtedly knew that he was hiding there and he needed to get out fast.

"I'm going to go through the window and get to the jungle. They'll have less of a chance catching me there."

"I'm coming with you," said Marian. Don Juan turned to her and gently kissed her lips.

"You can't. I'm sorry, Marian, but I can't let you do this. This is my mess to deal with. It will be far easier for me to do this alone."

She fell into his arms. It was the first time that Don Juan had called her by her first name. The way he said it was so intimate, as if they had known each other for decades and he was speaking his most intimate secrets to her under the shield of their covers. Marian felt tears rise into her eyes and he wiped them away.

"Trust me," he said. I won't let them take me. This won't be the end for us, Marian."

She kissed him again, passionately, not caring whether the roof collapsed upon them from the thundering footsteps that were fast approaching. The housekeeper let out a gasp and stuck her head back into the room.

"Now! Now! They're almost here!" she hissed.

Don Juan smiled sadly to Marian and before she could say another word, he leapt from the balcony and into the palm trees below. He staggered for only a moment as he tore away from the villa and into the vastness of the nearby jungle. Marian could hear the housekeeper outside the room doing everything in her power to get the men to not enter, but despite her best efforts, the doors soon swung open and Dr. Bartley stood at the entrance, surrounded by a group of men carrying automatic weapons. He looked Marian up and down and a crooked, vicious smile played upon his lips.

"I see that you are not the consummate professional you thought you were," said Dr. Bartley. "Where did he go?"

"I don't know what you're talking about," spat Marian. Dr. Bartley came closer, a cat stalking his helpless prey, the sinister smile still intact.

"Let's not play this game shall we? You've already made him take the bait, now tell us where he is."

Bait? Marian shook her head, trying to grasp what was being said. "Bait?" she repeated.

Dr. Bartley's grim widened. "Come now, Ms. Woolridge. You're smarter than that. We all know that women are a particular distraction for Don Juan, but you… you are the best distraction of all. We knew if we brought you here you would be so taken with you that he would completely let his guard down and make it easier to take him by surprise. I just… didn't expect you'd do your job so well."

Marian gasped. Dr. Bartley was using them both. He had clearly been planning to destroy Don Juan for a long time - and he used her to lull him into a false sense of security. Marian covered her face with her hands. How could she not see what was happening?

As if sensing her shame, Dr. Bartley came ever closer and put his hand on her shoulder. She recoiled but his grip stayed strong.

"All you need to do is tell us where he's hiding," said Dr. Bartley. "You can leave this place as if nothing had happened. No one needs to know about your meeting with him today. Things will be just as they've always been. Better yet, you can be the first journalist in the world to report Don Juan's untimely demise after his scientific team discovered how abusively he was treating so many women."

Marian was about to spit in Dr. Bartley's face and berate him for his lies when there was suddenly a loud bang outside the hallway. The housekeeper ran inside the room to take cover and several of the men, who had been assembled inside the room, scrambled into the hallway to see what had happened.

"Sir, there was a grenade!" said one of the men. "Someone threw a grenade down the hallway!"

The doctor let go of Marian's shoulder and ran towards the bedroom door. It was now or never. Marian turned from the men and sprinted off the balcony, hurdling herself into the bushes below. She heard a yell from above as the men suddenly realized that she was gone and she ducked down into the bushes, concealing herself completely as the men rushed above her.

"Find her!" Yelled Dr. Bartley, his voice ringing out over the sound of another grenade. "Corporate will have our heads if they find out we have loose ends!"

Before she was able to crawl out of the bushes, a hand clasped over her mouth. She yelped in shock, but stopped when she realized the hand was soft and feminine.

"Don't move," whispered a familiar voice. "Wait for them to run out into the hallway."

9

The fear immediately melted. Marian knew who was behind her. The hand around her mouth moved away from her and Marian turned to see Devon sitting in front of her, a large shotgun positioned in her right hand.

"Once they're down the hallway, we can get moving," she said.

A third grenade sounded from within the villa. The men above them scattered, leaving their position in the bedroom and finally running out into the hallway. Devon grabbed Marian's arm and led her out past the beach and into the trees that lined the edge of the jungle. Marian was running as fast as her legs could carry her until Devon suddenly stopped, her eyes on the trees around her. Both Devon and Marian wheezed from running through the jungle. Once she could catch her breath, Marian stood up and looked around her.

"What's happening?" she said. "Where's Don Juan?"

Devon sighed and reloaded her weapon. "He's fine," said Devon. "The others are leading him out to the airfield. They'll get him out of here."

"Others?"

Devon grinned. "You didn't think we were just going to let the bastards kill him, did you? There's an entire army of us - a whole communion of women who have been touched in more ways than one by Don Juan Velociraptor. Corporate doesn't care about him - they only care about the fame they can get from him."

"Who's Corporate?" demanded Marian. "Why do they want to kill him?"

"It's who the scientists work for," said Devon. "They want to control all government agencies from the pharmaceutical industry. Don Juan was supposed to tout their greatness, but he wouldn't do it. He didn't agree with the morality of some of their experiments. Instead, he…"

"Fucked everyone," said Marian.

Devon laughed in spite of herself and put her gun back in her pocket. "Yeah, he did. You're different though,"

“I bet he says that to all the pretty girls.”

Devon looked down for a moment before meeting Marian’s eyes again. She shook her head. “No, you're actually different,” she said. “Trust me, I can tell.”

The swell of excitement blossomed in the pit of Marian’s stomach, but this time, she didn’t try to push it down. She let it expand, flowing outwards into every part of her body, filling her with a sensation that was both joyful and erotic.

“Regardless, we have to get him out of here,” said Marian. “Tell me what you want me to do.”

The plan was simple. Marian would follow Devon as they made their way to the depths of the jungle to help get Don Juan onto the carrier jet safely. Some of the other people Devon had recruited, admirers and lovers of Don Juan, would create distraction for Dr. Bartley and his team. They were already responsible for the grenades - what other mischief could they create for the men who sought to destroy their beloved Don Juan Velociraptor?

Devon cocked her gun and they rushed out into the jungle. She could hear shouts behind her - a clear sign that the men had made their way through the villa and had discovered their path to the jungle. The occasional explosion and firing of a weapon echoed in the distance. The women were making it a fight, that was for certain. Every BOOM and fired shot was a confirmation that Dr. Bartley and his men had been delayed, giving them enough time to make it out to the airfield.

They reached the clearing and Marian caught her breath as she saw it open up to reveal the airfield. A wave of relief washed over her - Don Juan was standing in the middle of the airfield, beside the colossal carrier jet, his eyes fixed at the jungle. His eyes widened with elation when he saw Marian run out onto the airfield.

"Wait! Marian!" yelled Devon. But everything around her had already faded away and Marian was sprinting out onto the airfield. She was so ecstatic in Don Juan's embrace that she didn't hear the warnings from Devon, nor the shots that rang out from the edge of the clearing. Don Juan staggered, his massive body falling backwards as something grazed the side of his shoulder. He let out an enormous roar and a small group of women emerged from the carrier and caught onto him, pulling him up and onto the jet.

Marian stared in horror as the men rushed the airfield and fired a barrage of bullets into Devon. Their weapons continued to take aim at the carrier jet as Marian staggered on and the pilot began to prepare for his ascent. The sound of bullets bouncing off the metal around them resounded with a feverish tempo. For a moment, Marian doubted that they would ever make it off the ground, but as the engine below them roared and the carrier jet gained speed, the pinging of bullets and the roars of the men behind the weapons faded into memory. They were finally safe.

Marian was about to cry out in delight when she looked down and gasped - Don Juan had been hit not once, but several times. Blood oozed out of a series of fresh bullet wounds over his chest and shoulder, coloring his feathers and scales with a musty shade of burnt red and brown. She dropped to her knees and wrapped her arms around him.

"No," she whispered. "No, don't you dare die on me. Not like this."

Don Juan smiled wistfully and she could see through the smile that he was in a lot of pain.

"I'm afraid I can't control the outcome of this," he choked. "But even so, I want you to know it was always you. From the beginning."

Tears blinded Marian leaned in closer, planting a soft kiss on his reptilian lips. Don Juan gasped for air and as the carrier jet roared through the sky, Marian knew that with or without him, her life would never be the same.

10

It was a race against time. Don Juan was airlifted into the nearest hospital where he was to receive what could be a life-saving surgery. The bullets had lodged deeply into his tissue, the doctors warned. The operation would have to happen immediately, but there was no guarantee that it would be able to stop the bleeding.

"It's going to be difficult," the surgeon told Marian. "Probably the most difficult surgery we've ever performed here. But there's hope."

Hope. That was the only thing Marian needed to hear to keep her heart beating. She couldn't quite describe it - it was so insane and so unlike her to fall so completely, but in the hours when the surgery took place, Marian realized that the feelings of love had sparked on that first meeting and had steadily built into a brushfire of passion over the last few days. Even the women, Don Juan's eternal admirers, seemed to step aside to allow her to take the lead on the tender moments that would follow once surgery was completed. There was a deep, palpable love that all of them could sense, one that Marian quickly realized she could not escape.

She watched him sleep. Beside the blinking monitors and the chaotic sounds of the busy hospital rooms outside, Marian looked down upon Don Juan and realized that she was looking into her future. She had always been so scared of love, but only because she knew that the truest love would be unfathomable. In all her life, she had never wanted anything more than to see Don Juan's full recovery so that once he was released, they could begin their life together. It would be a story for the ages.

Marian suddenly frowned. Her story. The article that she had been laboring after, researching and poring over every day, wasn't something that would just go away. Her editor was expecting something, something that would break open the truth of Don Juan Velociraptor and let the world know that he was just another man trapped in a dinosaur's body. But everything had changed. She went into those interviews thinking that she had a handle over it all, but now she realized that the story she had aimed to write could no longer be written. That story did not exist.

Don Juan stirred in his sleep. Marian's heart skipped a beat. Would he finally awaken? It felt like he had been sleeping forever, but knew that the surgery had invariably taken away a great deal of his strength. She squeezed his hand gently and he squeezed back, the most tender gesture to let her know that he was there to stay. She smiled and pressed her lips to his.

She heard the door open across the room and looked up to see a doctor standing there, dressed in her white coat. The doctor smiled at Marian and seated herself across the room.

“How are you feeling?” asked the doctor.

“Me?” said Marian. “Oh, I’m fine. Just you know…”

The doctor smiled and nodded. “You’ve been through a lot. It’s inevitable that you’d feel very drained.’

Marian looked down again at Don Juan, caressing his face with her fingertips.

“How is he?”

“He’s very lucky. You brought him to the hospital at the perfect time. Had it been even a minute later…”

The doctor didn’t need to finish her sentence. The weight of what could have been pressed heavily onto Marian and tears welled in her eyes. She wiped them away quickly, embarrassed at being so overcome by emotion. The doctor thought nothing of it. She rose from her seat and handed Marian a box of tissues, which Marian gratefully accepted.

"He will make a full recovery," said the doctor. "It will be a long road - he's lost a lot of blood. But, once he gets enough sleep, time will do the rest. He's going to be just fine."

Marian could no longer stop the tears and she let them flow as the doctor looked on, her face a portrait of patience and kindness.

"That bastard," whispered Marian. "He killed Devon,"

"Who do you mean?" asked the doctor.

"Dr. Bartley. He and his men killed Don Juan's assistant. Do we have any idea where they went?"

The doctor shook her head. "By the time the police arrived, they were long gone."

Marian grimaced. Something wasn't completely right. She looked up at the doctor, at the calm, patient face that stared back into hers and she wiped away the rest of her tears.

"Devon said something before she died," said Marian. "I couldn't understand the whole thing but she said that Dr. Bartley and the men on the island had involvement with something called The Corporation."

At once, the doctor's face changed. It was a subtle change, a falling of the brows and a hardening of the eyes, but it was something that Marian immediately clocked. The doctor stayed completely still, but there was something in her demeanor that appeared to lean in, as if she were about to make Marian privy to a terrible secret.

"Do not speak that name out loud," she whispered.

Marian was taken aback. She opened her mouth to respond, but the doctor put up her hand for silence.

"I can't talk about this," she whispered. "Not here, not anywhere. It's best that you forget that name entirely."

"Why?" whispered Marian. "Are they still around us?"

Just at that moment, another doctor stepped into the room. He saw the two women talking and looked bashful, as if he had interrupted a meeting of the utmost importance.

"Sorry, umm… I can come back…"

"It's perfectly fine," said the doctor. "We were wrapping up here anyway. In any event, Ms. Woolridge, I'm happy that we've had a positive outcome here."

Marian was still fearful of the talk of The Corporation, but realized that nothing could be done at that moment. She beamed a smile at the doctors as they left the room and she returned her attention to Don Juan.

His eyes were fluttering - the weight from a dream. Marian

hoped he was dreaming of her, dreaming of the life they would lead together, of the future that she would always treasure. The sunlight peeked from between the hospital blinds and spilled out onto both of them. It was a summoning, a reminder that with love and passion, there could always be hope. Despite her days of fighting off the feelings she feared, she could no longer keep them bottled up. They would always spill over, like a cup too full, making her come back to him for more… everything.

And as she lost herself in the dreams of the erotic adventures they would have together, Don Juan's eyes fluttered open.

EPILOGUE

An excerpt from Marian Woolridge's article, *The Price of Seduction*

No one begins a story and thinks they'll fall in love. The idea in itself is absurd. For me, love was always something that was far out of reach, a distant priority in comparison to the career that I had been nurturing for decades. Sometimes, the world has other plans. Even as I write this, I realize the absurdity of it all - that I'd fallen in love with my subject, the famed Velociraptor who I had set out to prove as a fraud.

It was only one night. That was all it took for the passion to take off. Yes, he was *very* good, and yes, I knew that he would put specific attention into my body because of how dearly I'd tried to deny my feelings for him. I was expecting it to feel incredible, but I wasn't expecting what happened afterwards.

I think that we can thank Dr. Bartley. In a way, his drive to destroy his creation brought us closer together, and although he ultimately failed, it was exactly what I needed to realize how much Don Juan meant to me, and how much I meant to him. Upon his return from the hospital, we confessed our love for each other and made the decision to never be apart. Sure, it was crazy. I had many friends and family members tell me that what I was doing was not completely sound, but our hearts knew what they wanted. We tied the knot that last October, with those family and friends as witnesses, because they all knew that it was our happiness that mattered most.

I know why there are misgivings. Why should I trust someone who has such a colorful history of bedding every woman as an act of conquest? Why would I think he'd be loyal to me, or even deeper than that, how could I be assured that he wouldn't do the same with someone else? The short answer is that there is no reason. You can never predict what a person will be like in one year, five years, ten years, 165 million years. That is where the art of trust truly comes in. I have to trust that now that he is with me, he's here to stay, and in the same vein, he needs to trust the same with me. There will never be guarantees, but isn't that the beauty of relationships?

Despite his past, I choose to believe that he will love me unconditionally until the day I die. Despite my past, he chooses to believe that I will never throw him away if I become too busy or too tired. Any interspecies relationship is going to take work, and we are no exception. But if there's anything writing and researching this article has taught me, it's this - the world is full of wild and unexpected things. If someone had told me a year ago that I would be writing this from mine and Don Juan's home in Costa Rica, I would have thought they were insane. The world had other plans - just when you least expect it.

Besides, who am I to question the undying passions of Don Juan Velociraptor?

9 ½ Velociraptors

Elizabeth looked inside the tunnel and fixed her glasses that went far too low on the bridge of her nose. When she had only started to work in the lab she couldn't have imagined that she'd be seeing things like these, that she'd bear witness to dinosaurs in the wild and observe their life. At the start of this research program, quantum-tunneling technology was used to observe evolutionary processes happening, so they could make notes on what really pushed the changes. Once that goal was reached, it was time to look into each historical moment deeper. Elizabeth was busy with documenting and observing pre-historic times for a while now and her fascination with the long-gone population of dinosaurs only grew stronger.

Not so long ago a pack of velociraptors caught her eye. Before starting her work Elizabeth always thought that dinosaurs were vicious, only following their instincts and nothing else. After a month of observing, however, she started to change her mind. It was obvious to her now that each one of the creatures she was looking at using this amazing technology had its own personality, and its own struggles, but in the end, they all worked together to survive.

Blue seemed to be the youngest of the pack. Elizabeth was giving them names based on their looks and personality and Blue just had the tiniest hint of that color running along his back. He was always all around the place, helping the others, and teaching the small raptors how to behave.

Mary was always guarding a clutch of eggs, being one of the most fertile in the group. Others treated her well, always bringing her the best pieces of meat and that's how Elizabeth knew that they valued each other and their pack.

Hunter was the one bringing in most of the food. While raptors mostly could only hunt in packs, he could successfully bring in small mammals even on his own. One day Elizabeth witnessed him mating with Mary and it was a picture both disturbing and mesmerizing. It looked like a fight at first, but Elizabeth noticed that there were no wounds, no blood. Their noses bumped into each other as if they were kissing. Then Mary turned, pressed against the tree, while Hunter took her from behind, their screams loud. Elizabeth couldn't take her eyes away. It was clear that both raptors enjoyed it, that this passionate mating was something they both wanted. And, for a split second, Elizabeth wanted to feel it too, but she quickly got that thought out of her head.

The most vicious and unpredictable one in the pack was Scratch, but even being impulsive, loud, and sometimes aggressive he served his purpose – with raptors being small and sometimes helpless in the face of large predators, Scratch was the one to come forward and scare them away with his aggressive and irrational behavior. It seemed like he wasn't afraid of anything, which made the rest of the pack both fearful and respectful of him.

"Too bad we can't bring one of them here to get a closer look," Elizabeth almost jumped hearing a voice next to her. Looking into the tunnel she almost forgot that she wasn't the only one in the lab. Eric was looking at her with a smile, waiting for the response.

"Well, technically we can do that," she said, feeling awkward while he looked at her like this, giving Elizabeth all of his attention. "But we're not allowed. Which is a real shame."

"You're right," Eric said, standing even closer to her. Elizabeth wondered if he intended to be almost pressed to her side or if it was just an awkward move he made. "It is a shame. We could've learned a lot more about them if only they were here, in the lab."

Elizabeth smiled shyly, looking at Eric while he was focused on the raptors. She always thought that he was attractive, maybe a little too much for a man in the science field. Ever since Eric and she started working on the same project Elizabeth felt even more awkward in his presence. If she was completely honest with herself, she would've realized how big of a crush she had on him, but for now Elizabeth still just wished she could control how much she blushed next to him.

"Do you have any plans for the evening? Folks from evolution research want to go out tonight and they offered us to join. What do you think?" Eric looked at her with a wide smile, as if he really wanted Elizabeth to go with him, but she didn't know what to say or to do. She was so shy and never got along well with people who she didn't know. It was best to keep it safe, so others wouldn't make fun of her.

"I can't," she said, seeing the disappointment on Eric's face. She didn't like to see him like this, but it was too late to change her mind. "I wanted to finish some work, so I'll probably be staying late."

Eric moved away, his shoulders sagging.

"It's a shame," he said, starting to pack his things, making Elizabeth realize that the work day was coming to an end and she barely noticed it. “Just don’t stay too late, okay? I don’t need my partner to be tired during work hours.”

“I won’t, I promise,” Elizabeth said, feeling sad watching him leave. “Hope you’ll have fun.”

Eric waved at her before leaving the lab, the door behind him closing. Elizabeth was alone again, the emptiness that this brought her just settling in. She sat behind the desk, looking back into the center of a tunnel. The raptors were still busy with their lives, doing their best to be a valuable part of the community. Despite herself, Elizabeth felt tears burning her eyes. She could only wish to have that. Whenever she tried to connect with someone her shyness was always getting in the way and she couldn’t see that changing any time soon. If only she could be a part of something bigger like the raptors were.

Since she told Eric she was staying late, she might as well do it, but not without having a little fun of her own. In one of the drawers of her desk, Elizabeth had a bottle of wine that was gifted to her last Christmas. She wasn’t much of a drinker, so it just stayed there, waiting for its moment. It looked like this was the right one.

She pulled the bottle out and opened it, feeling the pleasant sweet smell. There were no proper glasses in the lab, so she had to pour some into her coffee mug. The wine made her feel warm, but the sadness didn't go away, it was just muted. Elizabeth still could feel it inside, eating her out, and it led to her pouring another glass. And then another. She didn't feel how drunk she was until it was too late. The wine was sweet, hiding the real amount of alcohol that was in it.

Elizabeth felt warm, her skin getting tight, and her heart beating fast. It felt the same way as when she was turned on. But she didn't want sex, not right now. She wanted a connection, she wanted to be close to someone, she wanted to be touched, caressed, and kissed. But there was no one there for her. And the closest she got to an affectionate partner right now were the raptors at the end of the still-open tunnel.

She had an idea. It was insane enough for Elizabeth to quickly disregard it, but it kept coming back. With no human wanting her, could she get the care and affection she needed from the raptors? Observing them for so long she did not doubt that they had all the qualities needed to make a good partner, but will she dare to break the rules?

Still hesitant, Elizabeth walked close to the tunnel. She remembered the instructions she received at the start of her research. A tunnel could bring someone from their time into the lab, but it wasn't allowed, since no one could predict the outcome of such an action. Well, with the amount of wine she had today, Elizabeth started to feel risky. She leaned down to the electrical box on the side of the tunnel, finding the safety circuit. Carefully, she removed the wire, seeing one of the sensors turning red. At least there wasn't an alarm that went off.

Still not fully understanding what her actions would result in, Elizabeth went to her computer to change the settings. She needed to focus on one of the raptors, so she'll only bring in one of them. Looking around, she had her doubts about which one will be best suited for this role. Still, Blue seemed to be the one who she could deal with. He wasn't too strong or too aggressive with strangers. Now there was only him in the tunnel and Elizabeth's finger hovered over the button. Was she really doing it? Was she really this lonely? And the answer was "yes".

Elizabeth didn't know what to expect, but the way Blue was transported into the lab wasn't going the way she expected. Here he was, standing on the grass, with his pack nearby when, suddenly, a tunnel seemed to suck him in and spit him out on the floor in front of Elizabeth. When he looked up at her, she could see the shock. It was to be expected of a creature that just went through time and space. And then Blue started panicking.

He got up on his feet, screeching noises coming out of his mouth, as he ran around the lab looking for a way out, dropping things from the tables. Elizabeth moved away, trying to be as far as possible from his teeth and long sharp claws.

"Calm down, please," she said, hoping that the tone of her voice will stop the raptor. Blue wasn't listening to her. He was panicking even more now, scared and confused about what just happened. Elizabeth had to calm him down if she didn't want him to ruin the equipment. Still scared of what might happen, she walked closer to Blue, extending her arm toward him. "Please, I don't want to hurt you."

Blue stopped in place, looking at her, his arm still up. He could hurt her with his claws, but Elizabeth was sure that this won't happen. She could see him better now, his green skin, his flaring nostrils, his yellow eyes. She was dangerously close now, but there was no coming back. She needed to calm him down and there was no other way to do so.

"Here," she said, putting a hand on top of his nose, caressing it lightly. Blue wasn't reacting yet, just looking at her. "I'm not bad, I promise."

He was the same height as her and Elizabeth could look him right in the eyes. Taking a deep breath, she put both of her hands to his face, letting Blue feel her smell. It looked like he was calming down, his breathing becoming slower and Elizabeth was happy to see it. He rubbed his face over her palms, inhaling her again and again.

When Blue moved forward Elizabeth got scared. What if he was still scared and wanted to hurt her after all? She was too afraid that he'll go into panic again, so she stayed put, waiting for what was about to happen.

His short arms went around her, Elizabeth felt the hint of claws on her back, and then Blue pulled her closer, his nose pressed against her neck. Her heart started to beat faster, fear making her freeze in place. Did he want to eat her? They preyed on mammals after all. A moment had passed, another one, while Blue was huffing and smelling her. When Elizabeth was absolutely overwhelmed with fear, she felt something wet moving over her neck. It was Blue's tongue. He accepted her.

"Good," she said, her voice hoarse. She put her hands on his arms, caressing them lightly. "Good boy."

Blue let out a weak clicking sound, letting her go. Elizabeth made a step back, smiling. All these emotions definitely helped her to get sober and now she was a little lost at what to do next. Right now she needed a companion, someone to make her feel like she belonged and that was exactly what Elizabeth planned to get now. She leaned to Blue again, pressing her much smaller human nose to his, rubbing against it, like she saw raptors doing in the wild. Blue let out a bubbly sound, moving against her too. She laughed, seeing that they made some progress. Elizabeth could already tell that this was going to be a good evening for her.

She spent the rest of the night exploring what being next to a raptor actually meant. She thought that she knew the way they acted pretty good, knew their reactions, but right now Elizabeth wasn't so sure. Seeing Blue so close and away from his pack made her question things. But not all of it was scientific. She also enjoyed seeing Blue's genuine reactions to the way she moved or talked. Her laugh was making him irritated, so Elizabeth tried to talk to him in a calm voice. He also didn't like it when she was moving her arms too much. What he liked, however, was when Elizabeth was turning so he could see her back. She was afraid to do so at first, in case he'll attack, but once she allowed it to happen, she very much enjoyed it.

Blue would put his arms around her again as if hugging her tightly, his head resting on her shoulder, the side of his face pressed to her cheek. It felt comforting, it felt warm. Elizabeth really felt like she was cared for. She could feel Blue's breath moving his chest against her back. Then he started licking her neck again, screeching noises becoming louder. And then she felt it. Something hard moving against her ass, fast and rough. She moved away instantly, and Blue allowed it. When Elizabeth turned around she saw it just for a moment – it was his cock, sticking out between his legs. Her mouth went open. Did he think she was one of them?

That she was ready to mate with him? Maybe it wasn't the best idea to repeat the things raptors were doing with one another after all.

"No," she shook her head, in disbelief. "No, this is not happening."

Still in shock, Elizabeth went to her computer, changing the settings of the tunnel once again. In a moment Blue was gone, taken back to his time. She could see him standing there, confused, until the rest of the pack surrounded him, sniffing and making sounds. They knew her smell now.

When Elizabeth lifted her hand to her cheek she could feel how hot her skin was. If she closed her eyes she could still feel Blue moving against her in a crazy desire to take her. Maybe, she should've allowed that… Elizabeth shook her head. No, this was a terrible thought, one that could get her in trouble. But still, even after leaving the lab to get a few hours of sleep, she was thinking about it again and again, until it wouldn't leave her head.

Once back in the lab, Elizabeth still couldn't stop thinking about what happened. She was doing everything on autopilot, almost not paying attention to what Eric was doing.

"How did it get there?" he asked, picking up a piece of equipment off the floor. "Did you drop it, Liz?"

"What?" she asked, looking at him as if she just got here from another planet. She cleaned everything once Blue was back to his pack, but it seemed like she missed a thing. "Oh, yes, it was probably me. Sorry."

Eric looked at her strangely but got back to his work. Today she didn't want to talk to him, to say anything really. She wanted to be left alone with her thoughts. Elizabeth hated to admit it, but in her life, she never had a connection like the one she felt with Blue yesterday. No words or awkwardness was needed, it was all based on body language. With people it was so complicated and often not worth the effort, but with raptors. Elizabeth knew that she made a decision before actually realizing it. Now she just needed to wait until Eric will go home.

When he started to get ready to go, he looked at Elizabeth as if he was surprised.

"You're staying late again?" there was confusion in his voice. "Didn't you do that yesterday already?"

"Yes. I think I'm getting too slow," Elizabeth sighed, trying to make sure Eric bought her excuse. "There is just a little work I need to get finished before I'm free. Don't worry, I'll be going home soon too."

"Just don't stay too late," he smiled. "And don't drop the equipment again."

They said their goodbyes and Elizabeth stayed behind, waiting until she was sure that Eric was gone to bring in the raptor. She looked at all of them again, still unsure if that was a good idea. Did she really was this desperate? Elizabeth already knew the answer. She was only able to wait for half an hour before getting too impatient.

Looking at the pack, she noticed Hunter standing far from the others. He was slightly bigger than Blue and for a moment Elizabeth wondered if she'll be able to handle him. She had an experience now, so it was supposed to be okay. She repeated the same procedure again, bringing the raptor to the lab through the tunnel. Hunter looked just as confused and scared as Blue was, but Elizabeth already knew what to do.

"It's okay," she said, getting closer and letting him smell her while staying away from his claws. Hunter still moved his head from side to side, until he took in the air, sniffing her. He got calmer, standing still while taking in more air. He knew her. Hunter smelled her on Blue and now he knew her. That was good, really good – Elizabeth would need less time to make her get used to her, so it all will be moving faster. “Yes, just like that. Come here.”

Elizabeth let Hunter get closer, as he smelled her neck, his nose pushing into her hair. She laughed lightly, but quickly stopped, knowing that they didn’t like this sound. Hunter was huffing and screeching while touching her. Elizabeth put her hands on his arms, caressing them, while still trying to stay away from the claws. It seemed like he liked her now. And she could attempt to do the thing she actually brought him in for.

Elizabeth moved away, walking to her desk, while Hunter was following her with his eyes. She could feel her body getting tense, fear mixed with desire just making her even more turned on. Will this happen? Was she really about to allow a pre-historic dinosaur to fuck her? Well, he couldn’t be worse than the boyfriends she had before.

She cleared the space on the desk, looking at Hunter as she pulled her skirt up, bunching it around her hips. Her panties were soaking wet in the front, so Elizabeth almost felt relief when she took them off. Hunter looked interested now. He smelled the air, his nostrils flaring and Elizabeth knew that he could feel her arousal.

"Come here," she said. She turned her back to Hunter, putting one knee on the table, and opening her legs wide. Now it would be easy for him to access her pussy, nothing standing in the way. Elizabeth just hoped that she was wet enough for him to get inside. "Come here, Hunter. I'm giving it to you."

Raptor slowly moved in her direction, while Elizabeth stood there, not knowing what to expect. She just hoped that Hunter won't get violent for some reason. Once he was close, he moved his head down, hitting Elizabeth's pussy with hot air. She froze in place, feeling Hunter's nose moving against her wet folds. She moaned lightly, enjoying the pressure over her clit. Hunter screeched in return. At least he liked this sound. He rubbed over her wetness, again and again, making her whimper and grab the edge of the table. Then it stopped.

When Elizabeth turned her head back to see what was happening she saw it. Hunter's cock was out now, looking slightly bigger than Blue's. The base was the thickest part of it, with some flesh barbs around it, while the tip looked smaller, with a big opening on it. Elizabeth's pussy clenched just imagining it being inside her. She was ready and she wanted it.

Hunter moved closer, laying his cock over her ass and starting to move it. He was trying to get inside her, Elizabeth realized, so she moved a hand behind her, grabbing his length and leading it to where his cock was so needed. All her thoughts went away after that.

The Raptors didn't have a rhythm, they didn't want to make it last. They were fucking fast and rough, greedy to leave their seed inside a pussy. Elizabeth realized it instantly – Hunter pushed deep inside her, moving in and out in an insanely fast rhythm, making her moan and whimper.

"Oh fuck!" she let out, grabbing the table harder, as it was shaking under them.

She never felt like this before, these raw fast thrusts weren't like anything else she experienced. The shape of Hunter's cock only added to that, making her feel overwhelmed each time he was pushing deep inside her. She moaned, her pussy getting tighter around him, as she felt cum spilling inside her. That was it? It only lasted this short? But Hunter didn't plan to stop. He kept going, fucking her even faster now that her pussy was wet with his seed.

With desire overwhelming her, Elizabeth took his hand and placed it on her breast, the light stubs of the claws only making her feel even better. In this position, with his cock still pounding her, Hunter stuck out his tongue, moving it over her neck, her chin, over her lips. It felt like he was marking her, accepting her into their pack. Elizabeth was a part of it now, her dripping pussy is another evidence of that. She screamed, an orgasm rolling over her body. It was so strong, and she felt so good, Elizabeth almost didn't notice when Hunter stopped moving inside her, but his cum was still filling her. Once he moved away, she felt it leaking out of her, covering her inner thighs and the floor. She definitely needed to clean up after this, Elizabeth thought, but her legs were barely holding her.

"You did good," she smiled, caressing Hunter's face.

With his cock still out and covered in her juices, she sent him back, watching as the rest of the pack surrounded him. Now they could smell her even better and Elizabeth hoped that next time he'll recognize her right away.

During the next few weeks, Elizabeth was getting closer and closer to the pack. Almost every evening she was staying behind, finding some excuse to be alone in the lab. When Eric would leave, she'd open the tunnel, allowing a pack member to come into the lab. Sometimes Elizabeth had to leave early and during those days or the weekends, she was devastated. She got so used to feeling the touch of a raptor, to allowing them to use her right on her table, that she was missing this feeling each day she wasn't getting it.

While Elizabeth was happy that she finally had this connection, that she belonged with someone, her work started to suffer. She was losing deadlines, and her performance turning not as stellar as it was before. One day, after another one of her fails, she returned to the lab to see Eric standing over her desk. He was looking at the deep scratch that was left there by Blue. Usually, Elizabeth would cover it with papers, but somehow he saw it and she was expecting some questions.

“I was just careless with the equipment, that’s all,” she said her excuse even before Eric asked the question. They both knew that there wasn’t anything shaped like this in the lab. He looked at Elizabeth with concern on his face.

“Are you doing okay?” Eric asked, coming closer to her. Elizabeth was surprised by the amount of care in his voice. “All these late nights working, the mistakes you make… I think you should take some time off, Liz. You should rest, clear your head.”

“No!” her reaction was instant, her voice sounding harsher than Elizabeth expected. She couldn’t leave the lab, she couldn’t be left without the pack. She needed them, more than anything else. “I’m sorry, I didn’t want to sound rude. I really don’t need it. Yes, I was out of the loop, but I’ll be okay. I’ll sleep all day on the weekend and will be as good as new on Monday, I promise.”

Elizabeth tried to hide the way she really felt about this offer and it seemed like Eric was ready to accept this excuse. He couldn't really do anything else about it.

"Fine," he exhaled, walking back to his desk. "I just want you to know, Liz – if something is wrong you can talk to me. I want to help any way I can."

She smiled, feeling warmth spreading in her chest. It was the first time in a while since she felt a connection like this with a human. For a moment she wanted to tell him everything, to confess that she did something horrible, something forbidden, but she couldn't. Even if Elizabeth was to stop, she would never confess to anyone.

While the day was coming to an end, Elizabeth kept thinking about it. Her work was suffering, she was locking herself up from the world. Could it really continue like this? Was it even good for her? By the end of the day, she came to the solution – as much as she loved the pack, this needed to stop. She was walking on thin ice already and if someone was going to find out about her use of the tunnel she'd be fired. She had to stop. Tonight would be the last time she would do such a thing. Full of determination, she stayed behind again.

"It's the last time," she said to Eric, as he looked at her with concern. "I promise you."

“Okay,” he said, still standing at the doors. “Get home safe.”

The door closed and it was time to say her goodbyes. Elizabeth activated the tunnel again, looking at all the raptors with which she grew close. She thought that it would’ve been symbolic to bring in Blue again. He was the first and will be the last one. Elizabeth focused on him, ready to see him face to face again, but at the last moment, something went wrong. Scratch pushed him out of the frame and, before Elizabeth could stop the process, he was sent into the lab, screaming and waving his clawed hands.

Elizabeth didn’t know what to do. She never brought him into the lab on purpose, knowing how violent Scratch could be and now there was no escape.

“Calm down, it’s me,” she said, trying to get closer to let the raptor feel her smell, but it did nothing. Scratch screamed again, moving toward her at speed.

Elizabeth ran to her table, wanting to hide behind it, but Scratch saw it coming. He jumped on top of it and then right next to Elizabeth. He pushed her against the table, her back bursting with pain at the impact.

"No, stop!" she screamed again, trying to cover herself, but it was useless. With his sharp claws, Scratch was slicing her skirt to shreds and at that moment Elizabeth realized what he wanted from her. The same thing that she gave all the other members of his pack. "No, go away!"

She tried to use her arms for defense, but just got a cut over one of them, blood pouring out. Scratch used his head to push her back, fixing her in this position, his cock already out. When Elizabeth thought that something terrible was about to happen, she heard the door opening.

"Liz?" Eric asked with shock, seeing what was happening.

"Quickly! The safety circuit!" she screamed, about to be taken by the predator right in front of Eric's eyes.

To her luck, he was quick. After another moment of pure panic, Scratch was sent to where he belonged and Elizabeth stood there, trying to cover herself.

"Are you safe, are you okay?" Eric was next to her in a moment, cradling her face and looking at Elizabeth with worry.

"Yes, it's just a scratch," she said, still shaking with her whole body.

“I’m so glad you’re okay. I can’t imagine what would’ve happened if I was late. I couldn’t lose you, Liz.”

Eric said it with passion and, maybe for the first time, Elizabeth actually saw him, the way he acted with her, the way he cared. She didn’t need raptors to feel this, she had everything that she wanted all along.

“I’m glad you found me,” she said, finally having enough courage to lean to Eric and kiss him. He answered her with passion, his tongue moving in the dance with hers. This was what Elizabeth wanted all along. And she didn’t need raptors to get it.

PREVIEW:

Triceratops & Bottoms

1

Erin stood on the balcony of her suite, letting the soft golden rays of sunlight bathe her smooth skin. She was completely nude, her firm breasts thrust out and her perky nipples erect. She closed her eyes and took in a deep breath, craving something deeper…more meaningful.

She opened her eyes and turned around. A draft of cold air brushed over her body and a shiver rushed through her. Just the slight tremor was enough to activate the nanobots, which drew the silk curtains closed and regulated the temperature in her room, making it warmer. Erin smiled and strutted over to her queen-sized bed.

The thing about the year 2122 was how luxurious everything had become. She had everything she wanted readily available. She didn't even have to snap her fingers like the ancient humans did;

all she had to do was think, and her needs would be fulfilled. In theory it was great.. but another thing about having everything you wanted was just how empty and unfulfilling all those things became.

This was the reason Erin decided to pursue her greatest and deepest sexual fantasies. With so much time on her hands, and nanomachines handling practically all work, she had the opportunity to pursue even the craziest reveries.

She settled herself on the warm bed and picked up her 'book of memories'. It was a digital device shaped like a physical book from olden times. It contained multiple exabytes of detailed data from all the wild sexual adventures she'd gone on over the years.

Erin smiled and went through each of the memories.

"I like to think I've done all there is to be done," she mused, tapping her finger on a date. She watched as a hologram played. She was in the middle of a group of bisexual alien races, locked in the most frenetic orgy she'd ever experienced. The blue-skinned alien people were insanely sensual, touching her from all angles; eating her up, making her scream, and fucking her like a slut. She felt her body responding to that memory, sending hot tingles rushing through every nerve of her body.

She'd gone around the various inhabited worlds, having sex with men, women and beings of all races. That was what she chose to do with all her free time. The pleasure always called out to her.

Sometimes she'd simply wake up craving sex and intense orgasms, so much that she'd just pack her bag and head off on a nomadic, hedonistic adventure offworld. Other times she couldn't even wait that long, and would summon a pleasure bot or holographic companion for immediate gratification…

The more she went through these memories, the hornier she got. By the time Erin closed the book her body was heated. She moved her hand over her chest and felt the stiffness of her sensitive nipples; going lower, she felt the hot wetness between her legs, moaning softly as she moved her fingers down there.

She wanted something more; something crazier, and out of this world. The last time she felt this way she went on an adventure to the farthest reaches of the planet and had sex under the splashing colours of the polar lights, and then she'd found herself on a spaceship leaving Earth for the outermost colonies. There, she'd engaged in orgies with a dozen alien races, giving her body to trembling orgasms and explosive pleasures.

Erin raised her fingers and pursed her lips when she saw how wet they were, coated with her sticky juices.

"Gosh, I need a good release," she moaned and fell on her bed, breathing softly. She watched the rhythm of her breasts swelling with each breath; the way her erect nipples poked out. The more she stared at them, the more the craving increased. She rolled off the bed and sauntered into the bathroom.

The doors hissed open as she got close. Adjusting the temperature of the water to a few degrees warmer and increasing the pressure, Erin closed her eyes and let the water do its thing.

I'm starting to find everything oddly erotic, she thought and let out a loud moan when the jets of water hit her most sensitive parts.

She stepped out of the bathroom half an hour later, more frustrated and bored than before. The last time she felt this way she'd travelled to an underground cyborg sex club, barely legal even now, hidden under a dormant volcano in Antarctica, for a series of encounters that had to be struck from the book of memories for fear of legal repercussions…

But what if that was it? What if there wasn't anything better than that?

These fearful thoughts made her uneasy. She lived for the adventure; a lack of it would make colourless and boring.

Erin decided to play with her new VR cocoon. She'd had it installed in a separate room a month ago, but she'd been too busy to bother testing it. Now seemed to be a perfect time.

She slid into the tight-fitting latex bodysuit and entered the womblike chamber. The lights dimmed all around her and a huge curved screen lit up. It spilt soft lights over her, inviting her in.

Erin put on the headset, fitting it snugly, and placed her hand on the main console. All she had to do was select whatever experience she wanted to have and she'd be thrust into it.

She could be an Old West outlaw, a superhero, a Greek goddess. The possibilities were endless, and it all felt 100% real. *Didn't it?*

"I'll just go for a more intimate option," Erin said to herself.

She entered an open world tailormade to suit her fantasies. It was full of fairies and magical creatures, and she'd oddly decided to add the option of dinosaurs. It was an improvised addition—she'd read something about dinosaurs recently, and it somehow popped up into her mind.

The VR turned out to be an intense affair, almost as good as the real thing. She slid into the Jurassic era and had strangely intense erotic play with different dinosaurs. The simulation was limited, she kept bumping up against artificial barriers, presumably because there were no detailed files from the primeval era. But still… she wondered why it felt…so good. So different from all the others.

She was a sweaty mess by the time she left the virtual world, in need of a burning release.

"If you enjoy this so much, why don't you go for the real thing?" the voice of her apartment said.

"What?"

A small screen came up and a message played out from her resident AI advisor. Erin watched with interest as it talked about a new scientific discovery: the invention of a literal time machine.

2

The more Erin learnt about the discovery, the more intrigued she became. She had heard rumors of the time machine, of course, but it had seemed only theoretical; not something that was about to become real.

Time travel was just what a free spirit like her needed. She quickly secured a pass to the unveiling in a couple of days. It was going to be a great day in the progress of humanity and technology, they promised, with applications in any number of industrial and medical fields.

"You had me at time travel," Erin said to herself, barely able to contain her excitement.

A couple of days later, Erin found herself at the unveiling of the new machine. Presentations were made on wide holoscreens; lights dimmed all around, immersing them into the images splashing on the screens as the man on the podium posed questions and dazzled the audience—including a wide-eyed Erin.

"Imagine what it would be like, being able to go back in time and relive moments you never would have been able to dream of. Time is like a massive thread interwoven across infinite realities. It's been a long time coming, but we did it."

A deafening round of applause echoed throughout the air. Erin was thrilled by the idea of going back in time. The present was somewhat boring at this point. She'd done everything there was to do; travelled all around, so it only made sense that the next step would be journeying to the past.

She raised her hand and drew the attention of the speaker. He pointed at her and she beamed, feeling like a nerdy girl at her convention.

"How far back in time can we travel?" she asked, and people around her nodded and mumbled; she'd read their thoughts.

"That's a great question," the speaker said. He went ahead to show a simulation of what it would be like to travel back to the past.

"The simple answer is this: you cannot travel beyond any time period more recent than the Jurassic period."

Murmurs washed through the crowd. Erin listened carefully, already picturing the wild Jurassic era, a little scepticism trickling in. What sort of adventure could one embark on during the Jurassic era? She wondered. She'd hoped to travel back in time to a crazy era, maybe have sex in the deep trenches of the WW1 combatants. Dangerous, sure, but it would be worth it. Besides, she would be safe because she had the gadgets to protect her.

Her mind snapped back to the moment as the speaker explained further.

"It is just for the fear of damaging human timelines. Time, remember, is like a thread. Snip the wrong end and it unravels hundreds of thousands of events, most of which would lead to the complete erasure of many of us."

The speaker paused for a second, holding their attention. "Imagine someone making a silly mistake and wiping off the timeline that would lead to the invention of time travel. It would be terrible!"

After the presentation, chances were given to volunteers to try out the invention. A lot of people were afraid because of the Jurassic era stuff, and the danger it posed; while others felt it would be safe to have other people have a go at it until all faults were ironed out.

Not Erin. She jumped at the chance as soon as it was offered, ready to time travel to the past and see what adventures she could have.

She was taken to a room where she was fitted with gadgets—force fields and rebreathers, and other useful items—and of course, her time travel belt fully charged and ready to go.

She was a little restless with excitement as they went through the procedure with her, and enlightened her on the safety measures and what to do when the charge became low—which was simply to return home.

"You wouldn't want to be stuck back in time now, would you?" the man asked with a slight chuckle.

Erin shrugged. "I don't mind, as long as it's worth it."

"Besides," she added, "I could end up being the first woman to invent some kind of alternate power source for my belt."

Taking deep breaths, Erin tried to get rid of the fear creeping into her mind. She was heading off into uncertainty. It could be dangerous, but it also promised to be fun.

I've taken risks before, Erin thought to herself. This would just be one of them.

"No risk, no reward, as the old cliché goes," she muttered to herself.

It was soon time to go. The instructions echoed around her ears as she put on her goggles and strapped on her time belt. She also took with her a camera, to make memories of the wildest adventure she would ever have.

Once the time belt was activated, it opened up a portal of light through which Erin stepped. The period and era were carefully calibrated, and off she went.

3

The light was blinding at first, and for a moment it felt like she couldn't breathe. Erin took a deep breath and exhaled once the light faded.

A rush of fresh air welcomed her to the new world. Her vision remained blurry for a few seconds, and her legs were wobbly. It felt as if she'd been spun around at light speed and at the same time, her body felt thin and weightless.

A minute later everything came into focus and Erin glanced up. She gasped when she saw the lush greenery surrounding her, and a majestic waterfall in the distance.

"Whoa, that's cool!" she said in awe. "I wonder where the

dinosaurs are…" she was saying when the ground shook underneath her.

Letting out a sharp gasp, she ducked and rolled behind a rock, her shaky hands reaching for the forcefield device on her wrist. She activated it and shut her eyes, panting.

Almost immediately a roar echoed through the air with tremendous force.

"That's certainly a dino," she muttered with glee, took a deep breath and finally managed to get out of her hiding place.

She took out her camera, keeping her force field on, and began her exploration.

It took Erin a few minutes to realize that having her force field constantly on depleted her power reserves, and she knew she didn't want that.

Taking a deep breath, and reminding herself of the thrill of danger, she took off her force field and exposed herself to the dense Jurassic landscape.

"Time to find the locals," she quipped to herself.

She cut through huge bushes and soon found herself in the open. The sky was a flush of bright colours, and the air was crisp and cool. But the main attraction came up ahead. Majestic dinosaurs roamed around, some in herds while others slowly crept through the distant forest.

From where she squatted, binoculars in hand, she got a breathtaking view of a brachiosaurus. It seemed to have its head literally in the clouds as it drifted slowly through the terrain.

“No one’s going to believe this!” Erin squealed in delight and took a few pictures. She also made a holographic recording for her book of memories. This would make a perfect addition.

She was still admiring the brachiosaurus, wondering what it would be like to climb on its back, when she heard the screech of a pterodactyl from up above.

“Holy shit!” she gasped and jumped back, cupping a hand above her forehead to shield her eyes from rays of sunlight. The pterodactyls seemed to fly in formation as they glided through the air.

“Okay, forget the brachiosaurus, I need to find out what riding one of those would feel like,” she said. “I just hope I get the chance someday.”

But until then, she thought; time for me to explore closer. She wanted to see the dinosaurs up close and get to understand their behaviours. She still had time—she checked to confirm—and adventure awaited her.

**

Erin spotted a herd of triceratops migrating across the plains. Fascinated by the creatures, she decided to follow them and observe their lives. They weren't aggressive—and she had her force field—so she felt safe enough to get close and take pictures.

"You guys look both majestic and cute," she complimented them. "And that's a hard look to pull off."

She sat on a rock and sketched one of the triceratopses. She'd narrow her eyes and take in its features, then smile as she put her stylus on her notepad and created the image. And in that entire time, she noticed how the triceratops stayed still, sometimes stealing glances at her.

It felt almost like it knew what she was doing and wasn't trying to ruin it.

"Wanna see what it looks like, big guy?" she asked with a smile, and it slowly moved closer to her.

She looked into its eyes as it got closer and felt oddly unafraid. Nothing in those shimmering orbs spelt danger. It was soon right next to her and she felt just how massive it was.

"Not sure I'd feel this relaxed around a Tyrannosaurus," she joked and to her surprise, the triceratops shook its head and made a laugh-like whizzing sound.

"Wait a minute, you got my joke?" Erin asked, surprised. She'd read about dinosaurs in history books and humans had always believed they weren't so smart. This triceratops laughed at her jokes and posed for her to sketch it.

And it was just so magical to look at. Erin sat with her knees together, placing the notepad on them. She wiggled her fingers and slowly reached out to the triceratops, careful not to scare it away.

"I came to experience your world," she whispered.

Her hand was just an inch away from the triceratops' face when the thundering roar of a T-rex shook the ground.

"Ah!" Erin screamed and fell off the rock when her new friend groaned and turned around, shoving her slightly.

The triceratops bellowed to the herd and hurried off to them. The roar continued, and soon the tyrannosaur showed up.

Of course she had seen that infamous saurian head, lined with teeth, in a thousand holos… but it looked so much bigger than any picture could have depicted. Erin stuffed her notepad back into her bag and got up, brushing the seat of her shorts.

She turned around and saw the herd of triceratops hurrying off. Swinging her gaze back to the T-rex, she gasped.

"It's going to kill them!"

She wasn't afraid for her safety but that of the peaceful

triceratops. Tiny bits of rocks flew around her as the T-rex marched his heavy feet on the ground.

Thick clouds of dust formed around the herd now trying to escape.

Erin leaped over the rock and ran toward the herd. She was well aware of the T-rex behind her, now charging at the herd. Her heart raced at a mile a minute, and the voice of caution in her head warned her to stay out of this. It was nature, and some animals were made to get eaten.

She shook the thoughts away, running as fast as she could, her feet digging into the dirt and grass.

“Nothing’s getting eaten on my watch.”

A large shadow crossed over her, carrying with it a rush of wind. She slowed down a bit when the T-rex’s large tail swept across her. She ducked and slid on the ground, splashing up water as she ran along the river bank.

The T-rex ignored her, easily outrunning her as it caught up with its prey.

Erin pressed a button on the device strapped to her wrist, and then she zipped over to the front of the herd.

“Woah, can’t believe that worked!” she panted, catching the herd storming toward her.

The T-rex snapped its large jaws at one of the triceratopses, narrowly missing it. While the herd ran toward her, Erin ran in the opposite direction, her eyes fixed on the T-rex while her fingers remained closed to her force field device.

The last triceratops ran past her—the one she'd been sketching—and suddenly stopped. It turned around and bellowed at Erin, calling on to her.

"I'll be fine!" she shouted. She turned around and saw that the herd were trapped by a mass of fallen rocks. They either had to turn back, toward the Tyrannosaurus, or wait for it to reach and devour them.

Erin held her breath, feeling the trembling beneath her feet. She was the only thing standing between the massive predator and the scampering herd. The T-rex was a few steps away now, roaring and showing off its menacing rows of knife-like teeth. She stood her ground, counting down in her head.

Just as it made to strike, she pushed down on the button.

"Don't fail me now!" she screamed and shut her eyes, bracing for whatever was about to happen.

The forcefield shot out and spread over Erin and the herd. A massive force exploded from it, sending the T-rex stumbling back. It roared angrily and snapped its jaws on the force field, unable to break through.

It gave up after a few tries, let out a warning roar, and ran away.

Erin switched off the force field, noticing a drain of one bar from her time belt. She exhaled deeply, sweat trickling over her forehead, and fell to her knees.

"That was close," she said to no one in particular.

But a familiar soft groan came up next to her. She turned and saw the triceratops. It rubbed its body on hers and offered her its snout as support.

"Thanks," she said and put her arm around its face, her fingers grazing its front horn.

The triceratops moved up a bit, helping her to her feet. She giggled when it lifted her a little higher, getting her feet completely off the ground.

"You're strong," she laughed.

It made a soft sound and gently eased her back down. Erin looked around at the grateful herd. She waved at them.

"I hope everyone is cool?"

To her surprise, the herd responded with sounds of their own. She was certain now that they understood her, especially her friend.

"Where's my backpack?" Erin muttered to herself, looking

around.

She retraced her steps, and the triceratops followed her.

“I hope the others won’t be mad,” she said softly, slowing down for the triceratops to catch up.

It groaned and she smiled. If only they could talk. It didn’t matter though; somehow, she understood what it said, and it understood her.

She found her backpack partially soaked by the river. Everything was intact.

Bringing out her camera, she took a few pictures of the triceratops.

“Let’s take one together,” she said and put the camera on auto. It hovered in the air as if held by another human, and Erin skipped over to the side of the triceratops. She placed a hand on the side of its face and grinned.

The camera flashed a few times.

“You’re a natural,” she whispered to the creature.

She frowned when she noticed a fading pink scar on the side of the triceratops’ face. She gently moved her hand close to it, caressing the scar with the tip of her fingers.

“Got into a fight, huh?” she asked.

It cooed.

"A T-rex, I bet?"

It nodded and she stroked the spot around the scar, listening to the soft moan her triceratops made. She found it weird that she thought of this creature as hers, not like she owned it but as a close friend; something that was a part of her.

Like love at first sight, except with an ancient creature.

4

It was a strangely satisfying feeling, bonding with the triceratops. Erin wouldn't let herself think of it as an 'it'.

"I'm going to give you a name," she said, sitting by the river, the triceratops nestling close to her. She enjoyed the feel of its body close to her, and the softness of its breathing.

"Let's call you…Cera," she giggled.

The triceratops did a playful shake of its head.

"Do you like it? I guess I'm not so great at naming stuff, but I think Cera sounds beautiful."

She looked at Cera and touched his face, stroking it lovingly. "As beautiful as you are, and just as magical."

Cera's soft groans let her know he enjoyed her touch. She stood up and wrapped her arms around his head, embracing him tenderly.

"Beautiful horns," she whispered and traced each horn with her fingers. "Majestic."

A rumble of thunder drew their attention to the sky.

"Hmm, it wants to rain," Erin mumbled, watching thick rain clouds slowly roll out. "I better get going so I don't get caught in the downpour."

She embraced Cera again and then, after hesitating for a second, pressed her lips on the side of his face and kissed him.

Cera's eyes widened and he let out a deep rumble.

He likes that, Erin thought, closing her eyes as she tightened the embrace. She was certain Cera felt pleasure from her touches, but she wondered if it was right.

She peeled away from the embrace and started walking away. The winds picked up, cold and fast, and a few drops of rain touched her face and lips.

Cera's soft noise made her turn around.

"Still following me, huh?"

Cera grunted.

Erin smiled and urged him on. "Fine, come on then. I guess I could use the company."

They walked together, almost forgetting the rain increasing in intensity all around them. Then, a flash of lightning cut through the clouds, and the sky opened up. Erin squealed when the deluge of cold water hit her.

"Oh no, I'm going to be soaking wet!"

Cera communicated with Erin with soft groans and nudges from his head.

"You want me to get on?" she asked, and Cera groaned again, lowering himself.

Giggling, Erin got on Cera's back and rode the triceratops. She wasn't sure if it was the constant humping as it ran, but her body began to tremble in a pleasurable way as waves of tingles rushed through it, heating her up.

Cera took her to a large cave where they took shelter from the rain. She was drenched and her clothes stuck to her body, accentuating her curves, and giving a clear view of her perky nipples and pink areolas.

She let out a soft moan when Cera snuggled close to her, his body somehow warm. Were dinosaurs cold-blooded, or had that been proven a myth? In any case Cera felt warm as a stove.

"I'll better take off my clothes first," she said, her eyes moving to the entrance of the cave. Rain lashed down from all sides, the cold winds whistling. "We might be here a while, and I think that's perfect since I won't be alone."

She made a fire the old-fashioned way and stood next to the burning yellow and orange of its flames. Cera watched her take off her clothes, her body bent over and her hand slowly caressing down her sides. She wanted to put on a show for him—longed to keep him engaged and mesmerized, that majestic creature—so she did some kind of stripper routine.

Her cheeks turned pink when she took off her soaked top, freeing her breasts. Cera's attention remained unflinchingly on her. She saw the intrigue glowing in Cera's eyes, like he was gazing at a hypnotic item. That was compliment enough for her.

She took off all her clothes, her body heated by the fire and the rising desire rushing through her body. She did a seductive dance around the flames, drawing the triceratops' gaze.

Her breasts heaved and danced, her body moving to a slow, seductive rhythm. She skipped over to where the triceratops was and put her arms around him, letting her naked body rub against his.

The moment soon became intimate between them, heated by the strong need for each other's company. Erin closed her eyes and listened to his soft sounds as her hands moved over his body; and she shuddered to the rhythm, getting a rush of pleasure from the connection.

Their minds seemed to become connected when she held his face and looked into his eyes. At that moment, everything seemed to slow down. The howling winds became soft songs in the background, and the lashing rain a chorus weaving around them.

Erin kissed the triceratops again, slowly this time. The tip of her fingers brushed over the side of his face, teasing him, arousing an ancient need in him. The physical contact sent sparks flying between them; heating up the flames of desire eating up their bodies.

The more she held on to Cera, the more she felt the connection deepen. The triceratops lowered himself, eyes closed, and slid into a world of euphoric bliss. Moans and groans and soft gasps filled the air between them.

With each stroke from her fingers, and kiss from the dripping softness of her lips, the triceratops found itself nearing the explosive heights of ecstasy, unlike it had ever felt before.

He soon let out deep grunts of satisfaction, brushing his face against Erin's body. She straddled him, trembling from the tingles of pleasure, and held on tight. She let her body move to the rhythm of Cera's ecstasy, and soon became engulfed by it.

She bit her lips and shut her eyes, grinding faster, feeling her heated sex become sensitive with every motion. Her arms tightened around his body, her moans louder.

The fire burning cast a shadow of their bodies on the wall of the cave, intertwined like two mystical beings locked in a beautiful dance of love and pleasure and deep primeval lust…

To Be Continued in

TRICERATOPS & BOTTOMS

Also available from Storm Crow Press

ABOUT THE AUTHOR

From an early age Lola Faust's fantasies and reveries tilted towards the baroque, the unusual, and the eccentric. Though she entertained curious private journals, it wasn't until she entered the Paleontology program at the University of British Columbia that her fantastic and romantic notions concerning dinosaurs took full flight.

While working towards her doctorate, Ms Faust began writing her signature saurian prose. Today she is employed by day at a leading university in her field, but maintains her anonymous and risque personality online.

Learn more at lolafaust.com!

Printed in Great Britain
by Amazon

56045210R00074